Ladybird Readers

Rebecca and Friends

Based on the Thomas & Friends episode
What Rebecca Does

Picture words

Rebecca

Thomas

Ladybird Readers

Rebecca and Friends

To access the audio and digital versions
of this book:

1 Go to www.**ladybirdeducation.co.uk**
2 Click "Unlock book"
3 Enter the code below

Notes to teachers, parents, and carers

The **Ladybird Readers** Beginner level helps young language learners to become familiar with key conversational phrases in English. The language introduced has clear real-life applications, giving children the tools to hold their first conversations in English.

This book focuses on talking about possession in statements such as "This friend has a crane" and provides practice of using words of emotion such as "happy" and "sad" in English. The pictures that accompany the text show a range of settings, which may be used to introduce topic-based vocabulary, such as "dig" and "lift", if the children are ready.

There are some activities to do in this book. They will help children practice these skills:

 Speaking    Listening*   Writing   Reading   Singing*

*To complete these activities, listen to the audio downloads available at www.ladybirdeducation.co.uk

Series Editor: Sorrel Pitts
Text adapted by Mary Taylor
Song lyrics by Naomi Rainbow

LADYBIRD BOOKS

UK | USA | Canada | Ireland | Australia
India | New Zealand | South Africa

Ladybird Books is part of the Penguin Random House group of companies
whose addresses can be found at global.penguinrandomhouse.com.
www.penguin.co.uk   www.puffin.co.uk   www.ladybird.co.uk

Penguin
Random House
UK

Text adapted from Thomas & Friends episode *What Rebecca Does* by Davey Moore. Based on the Railway Series by The Reverend W Awdry.
©2022 Gullane (Thomas) Limited. Thomas the Tank Engine & Friends™ and
Thomas & Friends™ are trademarks of Gullane (Thomas) Limited. ©2022 HIT Entertainment Limited.
HIT and the HIT logo are trademarks of HIT Entertainment Limited.
This version first published by Ladybird Books 2022
001

Printed in China

A CIP catalogue record for this book is available from the British Library

ISBN: 978-0-241-53371-0

All correspondence to:
Ladybird Books
Penguin Random House Children's
One Embassy Gardens, 8 Viaduct Gardens, London SW11 7BW

CREATED BY BRITT ALLCROFT

 HiT entertainment

 FSC
www.fsc.org
MIX
Paper from
responsible sources
FSC® C018179

water cannon

crane

digger

This is Rebecca.
She is happy.

6

Rebecca has a lot of friends.

This friend has water cannons.

Wow! Water cannons!

This friend has a crane.

Wow! A crane!

This friend has a digger.

Wow! A digger!

Rebecca is sad.
"I do not have water cannons,"
she says.

"I do not have a crane," she says.

"I do not have a digger,"
she says.

"What do I have?" she says.

"You have a lot of friends!"
says Thomas.

Rebecca is happy.
She has a lot of friends!

Your turn!

1 **Talk with a friend.** 💬

Do you have a digger?

No, I do not.

Do you have a crane?

Yes, I do.

2 **Listen. Put a** ✓ **by the correct words.** 🎧 📖

1 a I do not have a crane. ✓

b I do not have water cannons. ☐

2 a Rebecca is sad. ☐

b Rebecca is happy. ✓

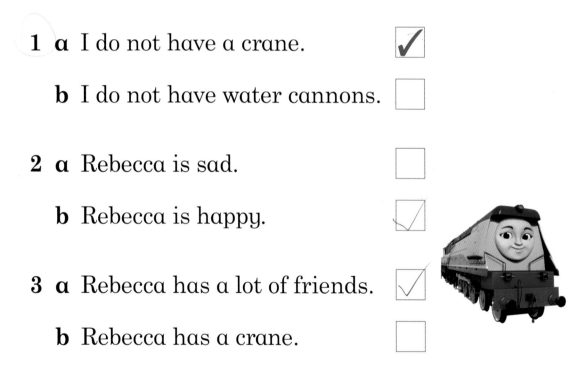

3 a Rebecca has a lot of friends. ✓

b Rebecca has a crane. ☐

4 a This friend has a crane. ☐

b This friend has a digger. ✓

3 Listen. Color in the words.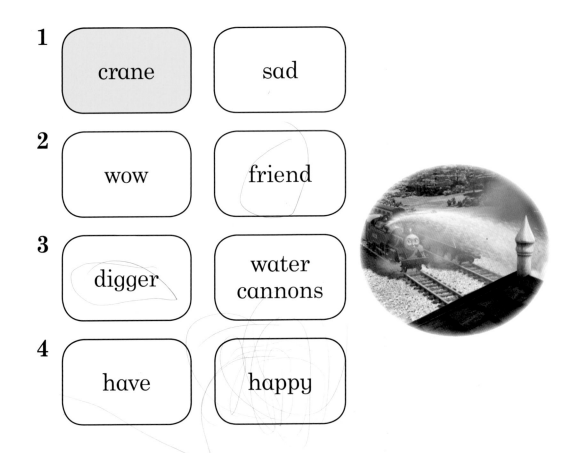

1

| crane | sad |

2

| wow | friend |

3

| digger | water cannons |

4

| have | happy |

4 Listen. Write the first letters.

1

friends

2

crane

3

digger

5 Sing the song. 🎵

Rebecca has a lot of friends.
What can Rebecca's friends do?

This friend has water cannons!
This friend has a digger!
This friend has a crane!
"Wow!" says Rebecca.

Rebecca is sad.
She says, "What do I have?"
Thomas says,
"You have a lot of friends!"